ST. PATRICK'S DAY AND THE LOST TREASURE

This book belongs to:

....

The Saddlestone Pony Listening School
Sinead and Strawberry
Roisin and Rhubarb
Conor and Coconut
Fiona and Foxtrot
Quiz book

The Blackthorn Stables Mysteries
January, February March, April,
May, June, July, August, September,
October, November, December

The Connemara Adventure Series
The Forgotten Horse
The Show Horse
The Mayfield Horse
The Stolen Horse
The Adventure Horse
The Lost Horse

The Coral Cove Series
The Riding School Connemara Pony
The Storm and the Connemara Pony
The Surprise Puppy and the Connemara Pony
The Castle Charity Ride and the Connemara Pony
The Shipwreck and the Connemara Pony
The Christmas Connemara Pony

Horse Books for Kids
P is for Pony – ABC Alphabet Book for Kids 2+
Listenology for Kids age 7-14
Horse Care, Riding and Training for kids 6-11
Horse Puzzles, Games & Brain Teasers for kids 7-14

Horse Books for Adults
Equine Listenology Guide
Dressage Training for Beginners
Horse Anatomy Colouring Book

BLACKTHORN BAY

Welcome to Blackthorn Stables in Galway, Ireland. Let's meet your new friends.

- **Emily** – age 9, has a grey Connemara pony called Basil.
- **Sophie** - age 9, has a black Connemara/Welsh pony called Daisy. Her parents run a guesthouse and pub.
- **Jack** – age 8, has a red bicycle and rucksack.
- **Conor** – age 14, has Rocky, a dun Connemara pony on loan. A cousin of Emily. Mum has holiday cottages.
- **Benji** – age 6, a smart, fox red Labrador dog.

- **Mrs. Ryan** – owner of Blackthorn Stables in Galway.
- **Inspector Oliver Oddsocks** – the local policeman.
- **Officer Katie Catchem** - the local policewoman.
- **Benny 'Bones' O'Brien** – village museum manager.
- **Miss O'Keefe** – the local librarian.

Chapter 1

Emily, Sophie and Jack made their way up the hill from the beach, chatting happily to each other. Emily and Sophie were riding their ponies Basil and Daisy, while Jack cycled along beside them on his trusty red mountain bike. Benji, their red Labrador dog jogged along with them.

Emily looked across at the village pub as she rode past it. Basil, her grey Connemara pony glanced at it too with a little snort.

Mr. Connelly waved at them from the tall ladder he was standing on, with lines of green bunting hanging from the roof of the pub.

"Morning kids," he called over. "You have a nice ride on the beach?"

"Hi Dad!"

Emily looked over to see her best friend, Sophie, waving at her father.

"We did thanks," said Sophie. "How's the decorating going?"

"Ah, it'll be grand by St. Patrick's. Your Mum has done a great job in the bar. Just this bunting to go, and then I'm off over to the library to help Miss O'Keefe put up some more outside the library."

"We can help," Emily piped up, as Basil, her grey Connemara pony came to a stop.

"Once we've taken the ponies back to Blackthorn Stables that is. I don't think Basil would stand still to let me use him as a ladder," she giggled and patted the Connemara's thick-set neck. Basil snorted.

"That'd be great if you can," Mr. Connelly called back. "There's a lot to do before the parade."

They waved again and set off back towards Blackthorn Stables, their conversation drawn to the parade. It had been the talk of the village for weeks now and the children were getting more and more excited with each passing day.

"I can't believe you get to take the ponies in the parade this year," Jack piped up from his seat on his red bike.

"You get to ride your bicycle too," Emily pointed out. "And take Benji."

Jack smiled. He glanced at the large red labrador that trotted along beside him as he peddled his bicycle. "That's true."

"I can't wait for the parade," Sophie sighed. "The bunting, the floats, the music and excitement…"

"The food," Emily added.

"Oh, I hope Mrs. White makes those green icing-topped cupcakes again, the ones with the chocolate chips in them," Jack grinned.

"Is your Mum making anything Emily?" Sophie asked. "We all know her pies are the best in the village."

"She is," Emily smiled. "Steak and kidney and sweet potato pie she said, and a roasted vegetable one too I think."

They rode on along through the village back towards Blackthorn Stables which was owned by Mrs. Ryan, a well-respected local horsewoman. It was the only stables in the village, and it did everything from lessons to pony treks for tourists, as well as being the local livery stables.

Mrs. Ryan even bred Connemara ponies and to add to the excitement of the parade, there was the prospect of foals too.

As they rode up to the little post and rail-lined driveway that ran up to the stables, Emily glanced into the closest field, its occupants grazing happily in the early spring sunshine.

"Do you think Magic will have her foal before the parade?" Emily asked.

"She might," Sophie smiled. "If it's a colt, Mrs. R should call him Patrick."

"What are you wearing for the parade, Sophie?" Jack asked his mind still on the celebrations.

"I have a dress, a big green one with a velvet skirt, and a load of green ribbon for my hair." She tossed her red curls with one hand, keeping the other on Daisy's reins.

"I'm going to put ribbons on Daisy too I think, and a green saddle pad."

"Hello there," Mrs. Ryan waved at them as they arrived up on the yard and dismounted, Jack propping his bike against the fence while Benji sniffed around the posts. "Parade route ride alright?"

"Great," Emily beamed.

"We did nip down onto the beach just past the library," Sophie admitted. "Just for a little canter."

Mrs. Ryan smiled. "Well, as long as you don't do it on parade day."

A couple the children they didn't recognise pulled up to the yard and climbed out of their car.

"Ah, looks like customers. We're going to have a busy week or two with the parade and all the folks descending on us for it."

She smiled and headed towards the couple.

Chapter 2

"Are you riding out alone?" Jack's head popped up over the garden wall, almost making Emily jump and Basil snort.

"Yeah, Sophie is helping her Dad finish off the bunting on the green and Conor my cousin has too much homework he hasn't finished yet, so his Mum said no hacking." Emily smiled.

"I'll get my bike, come with me if you like," Jack smiled. Emily smiled back and nodded.

"Mum," he called through the door. "I'm off out with Emily and Basil. Benji's with me!"

Emily vaguely heard Mrs. Lynch call an acknowledgement back through the open cottage door as Jack grabbed his ever-present blue backpack, shrugged it on, and fetched his red bicycle.

He wheeled it through the gates and stopped to give Basil a pat.

"I can't believe you live next to Mrs. Ryan's and don't ride," Emily shook her head.

"Eh," Jack shrugged. "I love the horses; I just don't love being on the horses." He climbed aboard the bike and smiled at Benji. "You ready?" The dog wagged his tail. "Where are we off to?"

Emily frowned. "I was just going to go to the green, but since you're here, how about going down the old coast road? It's closed for roadworks so there'll be no traffic."

"Right, you are then," Jack smiled.

Emily pulled a little radio out of her pocket and buzzed it. Mrs. Ryan's voice crackled down it.

"Everything ok, you left five minutes ago?"

"It's fine," Emily replied. "But I'm changing the route. Jack's with me so we're going to the old coast road. I thought I should say."

"Good girl," Mrs. Ryan replied. "Always file a flight path as I say, so we know where you are if there's trouble. Have fun."

Emily stuffed the radio in her pocket and they set off walking towards the old coast road that wound down the little cliffs to the beach below the village.

"You ever wish we had smartphones instead of radios?" Jack asked.

Emily shrugged. "They wouldn't work, they never do here, no signal, a bit pointless really."

"I suppose," Jack nodded.

"And I like the radios," Emily smiled.

It was a bright sunny, if slightly cool morning and Basil bounced along happily, Benji darting ahead, sniffing and then running back to them. The old coast road bent and twisted as it made its meandering way towards the shore. It wasn't very busy at the best of times, but it was silent and, Emily thought, very pleasant.

"Hard to imagine it being busy with goods coming up from the tiny harbor once isn't it?" she mused.

Jack nodded. "It is today. Hey, those must be the road works," he pointed to a hole that almost crossed the road surrounded by cones and tape. "What are they doing anyway?"

"Dad says it's something to do with shoring up the embankment after that little landslip last year, the one after that big storm. They're digging down and putting some sort of rock wall in on that section."

"Let's check it out," Jack smiled.

They headed towards the hole and as they got closer Emily stopped Basil and frowned. "What's that?" She asked.

"What?"

"I saw something glint by the side of the hole."

"Maybe someone dropped their watch or something?" Jack replied.

"Let's take a look, see if we can find it, give it back."

He waited as Emily slipped off Basil and they walked to the spot Emily had seen the glinting coming from. At first, it looked as if there was nothing there, but as Jack poked around something glistened in the sunlight. He reached out and picked something up.

"It's all muddy, hold on," he took his backpack off and rummaged through it. "It's here somewhere, ah," he pulled out a little bottle of water and washed the mud away. Emily stared as the shiny silver brooch in the shape of a serpent was washed clean of the dirt that had covered it.

"It's really pretty. And very unusual!" Emily said.

"It's not a workman's I'd bet," Jack added.

"Let's take it to Bones," Emily replied. "I bet he will know what to do with it."

Chapter 3

"My, my, it is a fine thing now isn't it," Benny 'Bones' O'Brien turned the little metal brooch over in his hand. He stood in his little museum, surrounded by an astonishing collection of things gathered from the village.

Emily loved the museum. No matter how often she went there was always something new to see. Fossils and old pottery were stuffed into cases, along with bronze knives and flint tools.

Old pictures of ships and village life were hung on the walls. There was even an old lamp from a ship hung beside a stuffed sheep that stared out from a corner display showing the things the village had once traded.

"Is it worth something?" Jack asked curiously.

"Aye, I should say it is," Bones nodded. "It's solid silver that. Nicely made as well. And it's old."

"How old?" Emily asked.

"Oh, well, I'd say looking at it, probably 17th century. Where did you say you found it?" Bones asked looking up at them as he put the magnifying glass he always kept in his pocket, back in its place.

"What is it?" Jack asked ignoring the question. "I mean, what's it supposed to be?"

Bones chuckled.

"Well, now there's a question and a timely one at that. This, my boy, this is the representation of a serpent, a silver serpent."

A strange look crossed his crinkled face.

"Why's that timely?" Jack asked.

"Because it's nearly St. Patrick's Day," Emily replied shaking her head. Jack frowned.

"She is right," Bones grinned.

"You can't tell me you don't know the legend of St. Patrick and the serpents?"

Jack's frown deepened and Bones chuckled.   He pulled up a chair and sat down on it, placing the silver brooch on a display case beside him.

"You mean you don't know how St. Patrick is responsible for driving all the snakes out of this fair island?   You don't know the Saint was attacked by snakes while he rested while fasting on a mountain and drove them into the sea?"

Jack shook his head.   Bones let out a short raspy laugh.

"Well, you do now don't you, my boy."

He looked over at the serpent.   "I suppose he must have missed one, wouldn't you say?" he laughed again, and slapped his knee with a hand.

Emily giggled.   "Except St. Patrick was way before the 17th century."

"That would be fair to say," Bones nodded.   "This one returned to Irish shores.   Now, where did you find it?"

"Down on the coast road," Emily admitted. "It was in the hole the workmen were digging up."

"Can we keep it?" Jack asked. "Well, not Emily and I of course, but the museum, the village?"

"I should think so. You really want it in the museum?" Bones smiled. Jack and Emily exchanged glances and nodded.

"Well, that would be great. I shall give it pride of place, put your names on the label as discovers. Alongside that dog of yours."

He rubbed Benji's head affectionately.

"And the pony no doubt!" Both Jack and Emily beamed.

"Now, if you will excuse me, I will secure this small treasure safely and have a look down the coast road myself, see if there is anything else down there that we should know about." He let out another short laugh. He glanced at the brooch once more.

"Silver Serpent, just like the cutter, I wonder...."

He shook his head.

"Come on then, off you go, you've got a story to share back at Blackthorn Stables this morning I shouldn't think. Why, it wouldn't surprise me if the paper didn't want to speak to you about this. It'll be the talk of the village, well, this and the parade."

Emily and Jack stepped out of the museum and Emily gathered Basil's reins from the little post she had tied him to.

He nudged her a little and she fussed over him before gathering her reins and mounting back into the saddle.

"I wonder what Bones meant when he said just like the cutter?" Emily mused as they wandered away.

"A cutter is a type of ship," Jack replied. "I remember from history class."

"A ship!" Emily smiled.

Chapter 4

Jack climbed up the little ladder that he had wheeled over to the shelf and began scanning the volumes of books in front of him. He glanced over at Emily who was standing beside a huge row of wooden cabinets filled with little drawers.

"What was the reference again?" he said, just barely loud enough to be heard.

Emily looked down at the card in her hand. "Em, DA 606."

Jack scanned the shelf for a book with the right code.

"I wish Miss. O'Keefe would digitize the library," he muttered, as he pulled the book out from its place on the shelf.

"I like the old card index," Emily replied.

She smiled at the bank of little drawers stuffed full of cards telling you everything you needed to know about a book and its location in the library.

Jack shook his head a little as he climbed down the ladder with the book in his hand.

"Jack Sullivan! How many times have I told you not to use my ladder," Miss O'Keefe whisper-shouted at Jack as she bustled into the room.

"Sorry, Miss. O'Keefe, we couldn't see you and..."

"That is no excuse," the librarian scolded him. "There are rules in my library," she pointed to a list on the wall.

"No loud voices, no borrowing more than five books at a time without permission, no climbing the shelves, no visiting the archives without a request, and no children using the ladders without supervision. What are you looking for anyway?" she asked, her voice softening.

"Is this about that brooch I hear you found?"

Emily smiled and nodded. "We want to find out a little about the town's history. Bones, I mean Mr. O'Brien, mentioned a ship."

"You know Benny O'Brien, with his tall tales!" She shook her head, her grey bun fastened at the back of her head bobbing as she did.

"We found a book about cutters," Jack waved the book he'd found and then frowned as he flicked through it. "Although it looks more like it's about how they were built."

"Would there be anything in the archives?" Emily asked.

Miss O'Keefe paused, a slight frown on her face.

"Well, let me think. I suppose you could check the old papers, but they only go as far back as 1800. The earlier ones we lost in a fire. They're on the microfiche machine. And I think..." she walked over to the card index and began rummaging through one of the little drawers.

"Yes, here you go, McIver's book, it details local legends and tales of the area, focuses on the sea. There might be something in that."

"Thanks Miss. O'Keefe," Emily smiled.

She smiled back a little.

"Mind, if you want to check it out, you'll have to do it under Jack's card. You already have six books out Emily, one more than I should allow you, but I know how fond you are of reading, so..."

She trailed off and a moment later disappeared behind one of the huge bookshelves with an armful of books.

The little village library was stuffed inside what Emily presumed had once been a large house. The rooms were now full of floor-to-ceiling bookcases, most of which had a table and chairs in them. They headed to the room which housed the book they were looking for. It was Emily's favorite.

A large airy room with high ceilings and two huge windows that allowed light to flood in.

An old table with green velvet chairs sat at the back of the room. They found the book and flopped down on the chairs, flicking through the pages.

"Wait!" Jack stopped Emily's flicking. "There!" he turned back a few pages and Emily saw the words *Silver Serpent* printed on the top.

"Wow, well spotted."

She smiled and started reading.

"The *Silver Serpent* is said to have been wrecked on the shores by Blackthorn Bay. An English Cutter, it is said to have been manned by privateers who had recently stolen goods from a large Spanish vessel, the *Santo Cristo,* a Spanish treasure ship."

Emily looked up at Jack her eyes wide.

"Privateers were basically like pirates," Jack said. "Just ones that worked for a country rather than themselves."

"And they're shipwrecked here!"

"Does it say what the treasure was?" Jack asked.

"Em" Emily scanned the page. "One sailor survived the wreck and told of Inca silver and gold. There's a reference too. Maybe we could look it up?"

"Pirate treasure!" A smile spread across Jack's face.

Chapter 5

Sophie scampered up the mounting block and swung up onto Daisy as Emily led Basil towards it. She looked back over Daisy's black rump and grinned.

"Mum says the guesthouse is fully booked for the parade weekend now," she said as she asked Daisy to walk away from the mounting block and stopped alongside Emily's cousin and next door neighbour Conor, on his pony Rocky. "It's going to be the biggest one yet Dad said."

"And we'll all be in it," Emily smiled.

"My Mum said the holiday cottages are full too," Conor chimed in. Emily's aunt managed three-holiday cottages on the far side of the green, opposite the pub and guest house. They were usually fully booked in the summer months, but it was rare for them all to be sold out this early in the year.

"Oh, I can't wait," Jack piped up from his seat on his bicycle. He rolled the bike back a little so the horses could move up alongside him ready to head down the driveway.

"Between the brooch and the parade, I think this might be the most exciting March, well, ever!"

"I heard about your find," Conor smiled. "A few of my friends from school were talking about it."

Conor, being fourteen, went to the larger secondary school a half-hour bus ride away, unlike the others who still attended Blackthorn Bay School. The idea that their find was known so far away made Emily feel a little fizzy with excitement inside.

"Bones is putting it on display this weekend," Jack chimed in as they made their way out onto the road towards town.

"I saw him this morning on my paper round. He's just finished doing the label for it."

"Did he really put Basil and Benji on the label?" Sophie asked.

As if in answer the red Labrador who was trotting along beside Jack gave a little woof. Jack smiled.

"He said he did, and you know Bones, he likes things like that."

The friends made their way along the parade route again, following the road past Jack's house and down through the line of stone houses towards the village green.

Emily's mum was in the garden tidying up and stringing green fairy lights through the still semi-bare branches of the lilac tree that grew by their gate. Emily waved at her and she paused.

"You off riding the parade route again?" she asked.

"Yes, Aunty Cara," Conor smiled.

"Those horses will know the route without you at this rate," she chuckled. "Mind how you go now, I heard a car come speeding in earlier, think it's some city folk come down for the parade. Your Mum was going down to the cottages to meet someone."

"We will," Emily replied and with another wave, they continued their way.

The parade route ran past the pub and sure enough, as they reached it Emily spied a large red car pulled up at the middle cottage.

Her aunt was by the gate talking to a woman with dark hair while a man was struggling with cases in the car boot, a mobile phone jammed between his shoulder and his ear.

"Should we go say hello?" Emily asked. "It wouldn't take long."

"Alright," Sophie nodded.

They made their way across the green, trotting over the green grass towards the cottages. Aunty Cara waved as they came across.

"Mind you don't churn the grass up before the party," she chuckled. "Mr. Doyle the parish chairman would have a fit. Oh, children, this is Miss. Flaherty. She and her boyfriend are down for the parade. This is my son, Conor, his cousin Emily, and that there is Jack and Sophie, her parents run the pub."

"Such lovely horses," Miss. Flaherty smiled. "Been ages since I've ridden. She came over and fussed Rocky who was closest to her. The dun nudged her gently and she giggled.

"Mrs. Ryan, she owns Blackthorn Stables. She does horse treks," Emily piped up.

"Down on the beach and everything," Sophie added.

"I might have to pop in," Miss Flaherty grinned.

Her boyfriend struggled past with a bag huffing and paying no attention to either the children or the ponies. He shook his phone.

"Dratted thing, why isn't it working?"

"There's no signal," Conor replied.

The man looked up as if seeing him for the first time. "What?"

"In the village, you almost never get a signal. No one really has a phone like that," he added. "We use walkie-talkies mostly if there's a problem."

"Or landlines," Sophie piped up. "There's one in the pub if you need it."

He shrugged a thanks and picked up the case muttering to himself as he headed for the cottage door. His girlfriend watched him and shook her head with a sigh.

"I had better help with the bags, nice meeting you all," she smiled and headed inside.

Chapter 6

Jack bit into a sandwich, before taking off a bit and handing it to Benji. The dog ate it in one bite.

"Nice of your Mum to give us a picnic Sophie."

Sophie smiled biting into her own sandwich and passing another bit to Benji.

"She said she was so distracted with the parade she made a ton of extra sandwiches this morning. Waste not want no she said."

"A picnic on the beach," Emily grinned, Basil put his head over her shoulder and snuffled around. "With ponies," she giggled handing him an apple core.

"Woof."

"And dogs," Emily added.

"Do you really think there could be a treasure?" Sophie asked suddenly. "Somewhere around here?"

"If the legend is true," Emily nodded. "But we don't know that yet." She shook her head.

The local paper had run a whole article on the brooch with a picture of it in the case. They'd even talked to Emily and Jack about where they had found it, which had been rather exciting.

"It was in that book," Jack said, around a mouthful of biscuit. "The ship was real enough, and the brooch."

"I was thinking about tracking down that reference in it," Emily nodded. "See if we can learn more."

"I can request the book if you like," Conor said. "From the library next to my school. You can ask them to get you any book."

"Thanks, that would be great," Emily smiled.

"Who's that?" Sophie looked along the beach. They all followed her gaze. A man was walking towards them from the direction of the coast road.

Tall and thin, with a mountain of red hair. He waved as he approached. "Good morning."

"Hi," Conor replied.

"Fine day for a picnic," the red-haired man smiled.

Benji, normally keen to meet anyone encountered gave a little growl and huddled beside Jack, his tail low and stiff.

"Someone doesn't want to share his picnic," the man joked.

Jack glanced at Benji, he didn't normally act like that around people, but then again, he did love food too.

"A lovely place you all have here, so peaceful," the man sighed.

"Are you here visiting?" Sophie asked.

"Indeed, I am, I checked into the guest house this morning. My name is Michael, Michael O'Leary. My family comes from these parts; I'm trying to find out about them. For one ancestor in particular. I found his journal in my late father's possessions and feel compelled to see where he came from.

And I am glad I did. I hear there's to be a parade and everything for St. Patrick's. So I couldn't have timed my visit better if I had tried!"

"Have you found anything yet, about your ancestors?" Conor asked.

"Not so much no, but then I've only been here one morning. Any ideas where I could start?"

"There's the museum," Jack said. "Bones, Mr. O'Brien, everyone calls him Bones, he keeps the place, and knows almost everything about the village and its history."

"Sounds like a great place to start," Michael smiled. "Thank you very much."

"There's the parish church too," Emily put it.

"It's pretty small, up on the hill not far past the stables, er, Blackthorn Stables. You can't miss it. Father Patrick is up there most days; he might be able to help if your ancestors were buried up there. Or if you would like to see the graves or anything."

"Now that would be something," Michael smiled. "Seeing where my ancestor's final resting place is. I will do that. I am very glad I ran into you all."

He made to turn away and Emily added. "There's always the library too. It's got a lot on local history and Miss. O'Keefe has old newspapers as well as a few archives. It's in one of the large old houses, right by the beach there," Emily pointed up to the library.

"An interesting old building that," Michael mused. "You wouldn't happen to know what it was before it was a library?"

Emily frowned. She'd never really thought about it before. She shook her head. "Sorry, no, I think the building next door was a parochial house at one point, but it was repurposed years ago and now it's our school."

"A whole school?"

"There's only a handful of kids in the whole village," Conor replied. "We have a lot of mixed-age classes, right up to seniors."

"Well, it looks like I have a lot to explore," Michael smiled at them and waved. "My thanks again." He headed away across the beach towards the edge of the village and the old library.

"He seemed nice," Sophie said and then giggled as Daisy nudged at her.

Chapter 7

The sun was beginning to dip low in the sky when the kids trooped back past the library, the ponies' unshod hooves making soft noises in the quiet evening light. Emily glanced back at the beach, the golden sun making the sand look peach.

"I wish we could have watched the sunset," she sighed. "It's my favourite time of day."

"It is pretty," Sophie admitted.

"Yeah, but your Mum would be really mad if we stayed and rode home in the dark with no flashlights," Conor pointed out.

"I have a few in my bag, I think," Jack frowned.

Sophie giggled. "And biscuits, and a hoof pick, and the kitchen sink."

"Always be prepared, that's what Grandpa says," Jack replied.

Emily smiled. Jack's grandpa Joe was always telling them stories of his days in the navy and how he always had to be prepared, and Jack had accordingly packed his sturdy rucksack with a range of useful things.

"Don't tease," Conor said. "Jack's bag has rescued us more than once."

"I know," Sophie smiled over at Jack. "But it seems bottomless!"

They plodded up past the museum towards the pub, the sun sinking as they wandered along. They saw the pub door swing open and someone walk out, a phone pressed to their ear.

It was an odd enough sight for all of them to notice. Emily glanced over at Conor who stared at the figure as it flitted down the little alleyway at the side of the pub.

"Why's he going down there?" Conor asked.

There were several little alleys dotted along the main strip of the village. They were narrow and cobbled, used mostly to get to the little yards, gardens and outbuildings behind.

"I don't know," Sophie frowned. "It's not really the weather to sit in the garden. The grass back there is still all soggy."

As they wandered closer Emily could hear a man's voice. They all knew it was wrong to eavesdrop, but the man was speaking so loudly it was hard not to.

"No, no, wait, the signal here is awful. Yes, hello. It's me again. No, no, everything is NOT fine." He paused. "No, I told you, I don't have it yet. Yes, yes I can get it, but...argh. Dratted signal"

Sophie glanced over at Emily. "What is he talking about? Do you think....?" she whispered.

"I wonder who he's talking to?" Conor mused as they slowly made their way past the pub.

The door swung open and Miss. Flaherty appeared. She smiled at the children. "Well, hello."

"Hi," Sophie, who was the closest, replied.

"Lovely evening for a pony ride," she smiled again. "You wouldn't happen to have seen Liam, my boyfriend, would you? He disappeared just as we had finished dinner, said he had an urgent phone call."

"We saw someone go down the side of the pub," Conor answered.

"Thanks," she shook her head and smiled. "I better go tell him that I paid for the meal so he isn't worried.

She waved at them as she headed toward the little alley and the children carried on up the road quietly. Jack paused a little as Benji sniffed around a plant pot. He heard Mr. Quinn still on the phone, almost sound panicked as his wife appeared.

"That's odd Benji," he said to the dog.

"Woof," Benji agreed, solemnly.

Chapter 8

Emily rushed down the street towards the pub, Conor right behind her. Sophie had called them all early that morning saying something was going on at the museum. She'd woken up to the sound of the two village police officers, Katie Catchem and Oliver Oddsocks, both astride their bicycles, rushing down the street.

"I'm fairly sure they went to the museum," Sophie had said on the phone. "You get Conor, I'll call Jack."

"Be there in ten minutes," Emily had replied and hung up before pulling on her jumper and racing to fetch her cousin from next door.

Jack and Benji had arrived on his red bicycle by the time Conor was dressed and they'd rushed together towards the museum, picking up Sophie on the way.

"I wonder what's happened?" Conor huffed.

"Has to be bad for both Inspector Oddsocks and Katie to be there," Emily replied.

The police officers' bikes were still pushed up against the wall by the museum, and a small crowd of villagers was beginning to form on the street opposite when the children arrived. Emily smiled, it was always the same in the village when something happened. People gathered but not too close. They never wanted it to look like they were being nosey when they were. She spotted Bones by the door and waved to him. He waved them forward.

"What's happened?" Jack asked.

"A break in, unfortunately," Bones nodded. "Someone came in last night and stole the silver serpent brooch right out from the case."

"What!" Emily exclaimed.

Bones nodded sadly. "Tis true. I heard the alarm go off from my place." He glanced a few doors down to his own little home. "I called the police and rushed over, but by the time we got here it was gone."

"Did they take anything else?" Conor asked.

"Not a thing my boy, not a thing. Targeted I say it was, targeted." Bones shook his head sadly.

"Morning children," Oliver Oddsocks looked down at them. He was a tall man, maybe the tallest in the village, who always wore his uniform stiffly pressed and his boots extra shiny.

"Now then, I don't suppose any of you saw anything odd about this morning, did you? Maybe a strange car or someone driving about?"

Emily, Conor, and Jack shook their heads, but Sophie paused. "I, I did hear something, before I heard you and Katie, I mean Officer Catchem, on your bikes."

"Yes?"

"Well, I thought it was a guest. Someone was moving around the pub, in the back I think, where the garden is. My room's at the side, by the alleyway, so I hear everything from the front and the back."

"And you thought it was a guest?"

"The guest house's full," Sophie nodded. "And a few of the guests get up early. Mum leaves a key on the latch in the kitchen so they can go out if they like. One of them is a photographer. She wanted to take pictures of the parade, but she likes to photograph the beach at dawn too."

"And her name is?"

"Green, Caitlin Green, she's over here on holiday. I don't think she'd steal the brooch though, she doesn't seem the type." Sophie added.

"No, but she might well have seen something if she's an early riser." He took a deep breath and looked over his shoulder at Katie.

"I'm heading over to the guest house, I'll speak to them about if they saw anything. Will you finish up here?"

"I will of course," Katie grinned over at him.

"Can I clean up afterwards?" Bones asked glancing at some glass on the floor.

"Yes, yes that's fine." Oliver nodded. "I suspect they came in through the back window. It's a bit of a mess back there too."

"I have some boards I can put up," Bones nodded.

The children filed out following Inspector Oddsocks. He mounted his bike and peddled away. Almost without thinking the children fell into step beside each other.

"Maybe we should have told Inspector Oddsocks about that Quinn guy," Jack said after a few moments.

"He was down the side of the pub last night; he was definitely up to something and he said he didn't have 'it', yet!"

"It's not much to go on," Sophie replied.

"We should keep an eye on him though," Conor added. "And we better get ready for school, or we'll be late."

Chapter 9

The children cantered along the sandy beach back towards the village. The whole place was now aware of the missing brooch and rumour was rife. Even their lessons that day had seemed distracted somehow by the event, as if Miss. Murphy's mind was only half in the classroom, the other half wondering about the theft. Most people assumed someone must have come into town at nighttime to steal it after seeing the article in the paper, but the children were still not convinced that Mr. Quinn wasn't involved.

"His girlfriend is nice," Sophie said as they drew to a walk."

"Doesn't mean he is," Jack huffed as he caught up, the bicycle's tires leaving a mottled trail in the firm sand by the shore. Benji ran ahead of them, bouncing in and out of the surf.

The labrador loved nothing more than running on the sand and often darted ahead of them to splash around in the sea.

Conor shook his head. "I still don't think we can say anything to Inspector Oddsocks, not without more than him acting a little strangely and having an odd phone call. He'd laugh at us."

They headed up the sand dunes back towards the road. As they reached it, Miss. O'Keefe popped her head out of the door.

"I heard what happened at the museum. I'm sorry, I know you were pleased about finding that brooch." She shook her head. "Is Mr. O'Brien alright?"

"I think so," Emily smiled.

"To think, he was only here yesterday getting books about it."

"About the brooch?" Emily frowned.

"So he said, although the books he took..." she shook her head. "More local legends than fact. You know I like a good story, fantasy, and drama, but he takes it all so seriously. Still, it'll have been a shock. You tell him if he needs anything to stop by. I heard he has a broken window and I have some old shutters we took out when we renovated, if he wants them."

"We'll tell him," Conor smiled.

They headed past their schoolhouse and up to the museum.

Bones was sitting on the front step, a licorice stick hanging out of his mouth. He waved as they pulled up.

"Nice ride?"

"Yes thanks," Conor smiled. "Miss. O'Keefe wanted us to tell you she has some old shutters if you need them to block up the back window that was smashed."

"Ah, that's ok, I've seen to it already, but I'll thank her."

"She said you got some books out, about the brooch," Emily added.

"Yes, I did indeed," Bones shook his head sadly. "I wanted to make a big panel all about it and the legend of the ship that I think it came from."

"The Silver Serpent," Emily added.

Bones smiled. "So, you've heard of her."

"Actually, you said her name," Emily smiled. "When we were here. I just found an article that said she was a ship, a wrecked one, around here."

"It's a true story, so they say. One day a privateer vessel, pirates for the crown of England, they seized a Spanish vessel that was loaded with gold and silver. It was part of a ransom taken from the Incans by Pizarro himself." Bones eyes danced as he fell into telling the story.

"Only, the Spanish on the ship, they told the English that the treasure be cursed, and that anyone who sought it would find misfortune and bad luck. They claimed that if it was held by a man, that man would be forever doomed to misfortune.

But the English thought it was the Spanish trying to keep the gold for themselves. So they stripped the ship of the loot and along with it the key to the chest it was in. A Silver Serpent.

They saw that as a good omen, a key to the treasure the same as their ship's name. Surely that would mean good luck, not misfortune. But just two nights later, as they were passing this very shoreline the winds picked up, howled along the coast, and tossed their ship like a cork.

The ship was smashed against the rocks by the headland of Blackthorn Bay. Only one man struggled ashore, and beside him was tossed the treasure and the key, as if the sea herself didn't want it."

"What happened then?" Jack asked his eyes wide.

"Now that," Bones stood up a little stiffly.

"That is a mystery. That sailor, he told his tale to the locals, and it was written down in the local legends, but what became of the treasure is lost to history.

Pizzaro's ransom though, that is a well-known tale, plenty of folks searched for that treasure, but none ever returned. If even a part of it was on the Silver Serpent, I could see why that sailor would leave it where it was."

Chapter 10

Emily, Jack, and Sophie skipped out of school and headed next door to the library. Miss. O'Keefe looked up at them over her glasses and waved at them as they trooped inside.

"Straight from school to the library! I wonder what could have fascinated you all so much," she chuckled.

"We heard about the treasure from Bones," Jack said.

"Oh, not that old tale." She shook her head and closed the book she was reading.

"You've heard about it?" Sophie asked.

Miss O'Keefe looked around the shelves of books surrounding them. "I know my books," she said.

"But you don't believe it, the tale I mean?" Emily added.

Miss. O'Keefe sighed.

"Mr. O'Brien believes, or would have you believe that every myth, legend and folk tale is based on truth. I happen to think they're based on a pinch of salt. Nice stories they may be and wonderful for imagination, but that's all. Besides, you don't want to go around telling folk there may be treasure about, we'd be overrun!"

"She has a point," Sophie said. "About being overrun I mean."

"We can still look though," Jack pointed out.

"Where would we look?" Emily asked Miss O'Keefe. "If we wanted to learn more about the legend that is. The truth."

Miss. O'Keefe frowned. "The truth," she nodded.

"Well, I'd say if it's the truth you're looking for, you should start in the archives.

I've a ton of stuff down there to trawl through, though I doubt you'll find much about treasure and shipwrecks. Still..." she bit her lip. "Maybe we could help each other."

"What do you mean?" Jack asked.

"Well, to be honest with you children I have so much work on keeping the library clean and tidy, the books checked out and in, I haven't had a lot of time to go over what's in the archives and catalog it. I took in a lot of old documents, books and journals when next door was converted into the school. They used to belong to various priests and the church. You're welcome to go through what's there, and maybe you could help me by recording what you find as you go."

Emily's eyes lit up, but Sophie sighed. "Come on Sophie, it'll be great!"

Sophie let her bag slide off her shoulder and let out a little huff as she dragged it along behind her following Jack, Emily, and Miss. O'Keefe towards the archive room.

A little while later Sophie looked up from the book that she was neatly writing details of documents in and sighed. "I feel like we've been here for hours!"

"We've been here forty-five minutes," Jack replied not even looking up from the book he was leafing through.

"This one's a register of household goods from," he paused and turned a page. "Erm I think that says Father Kelly."

Sophie scribbled it down in the book. Emily pulled another slightly dusty box from a shelf and opened it up. "Maybe we should target boxes that look like they're the right age. This one's from the fifties, too late for our shipwreck."

"Agreed," Jack nodded.

"And let's only do fifteen more minutes," Sophie added. "I'd like to ride Daisy."

Emily nodded. "Me too. Ok, fifteen minutes."

She stuffed the box back and pulled out another one. She opened the flaps and stared at the leather-bound books inside. She slipped one out and opened it up.

"This one's a journal. Hey, listen to this." She read out loud from the book.

"I have arrived at my new lodgings to discover the rectory is next to the village tavern." Emily looked up at Jack.

"Several times last night I observed sailors wandering from the port past my front door and into the public house. I admit to being worried I would get little sleep, but the walls have proven thick."

"Wait," Jack frowned. "You mean the library used to be a tavern?"

"That's what it says," Emily nodded.

"Whose journal is that?" Jack asked.

Emily turned the book trying to see and as she did a slip of paper slipped out and fluttered to the floor. Jack scooped it up and frowned.

"What is it?" Sophie asked suddenly a little more interested. "I can't tell, it's all faded and the writing is all loopy."

Emily took it from him and stared at the paper. "I can't make out much but...."

"What?"

"Well, doesn't this word look like treasure?" she said.

Jack's mouth dropped open. "It does, and that looks like a tunnel."

"And basement," Emily added. "I think this says hidden by the beach road."

They looked at each other. Jack took the slip of paper, folded it carefully, and stuffed it in his pencil tin.

"What are you doing?" Emily asked.

"We don't want whoever took the brooch to find this. It's safest with us."

Chapter 11

Emily slipped Basil's saddle over his back and patted him before reaching to do up his girth. As she bent to retrieve the wide green girth from under his grey belly, she noticed Inspector Oddsocks coming up the driveway to the stables on his bicycle.

She girthed up and glanced over at Sophie, but it was clear she'd already seen the policeman.

Inspector Oddsocks pulled up by the little patch of concrete with its overhanging roof and propped his bicycle against the fence next to the bicycle.

"Afternoon girls, Jack," he nodded at them. Benji wandered across and sniffed at the blue leg of his trousers and the policemen bent down patting his head.

"You haven't seen Mrs. Ryan around, have you?"

"She's in the big barn," Sophie replied. "She'd getting ready to lead a tourist trail ride."

"Would you happen to know where they're headed, or if she's led any other rides out the past few days?"

"Today's ride is up through the woods around the back of the church," Sophie replied.

"It has a good view of the coastline and a nice trot, or canter." Oddsocks nodded. "I'm not sure about other rides."

"There was one yesterday," Emily piped up. "Down to the beach past the library, along it, up the coast road and back. May we ask why?"

"You may," the policeman nodded. "Especially since I'm going to ask you the same thing I'm going to ask Mrs. Ryan."

"What's that?" Jack asked rubbing Benji's ears.

"If you've spotted anything strange down on the beach lately."

Emily frowned. "What sort of strange things?"

"Lights," Oddsocks replied. "I've had several folks call me up about lights down on the beach and by the coast road around the same time you found the brooch.

I thought it was just someone out for a walk. And I'll admit I wasn't too bothered, if someone wants to go out in the night who am I to stop them, but..."

"But?" Emily asked.

"Well, seems someone found a hidden metal detector in a plastic bag down by the coast path while they were out walking their dog.

Their dog found it, sniffing about. It just seems a bit strange. Why hide the thing, why not take it home? Seemed odd. And with the brooch being stolen, I thought I'd dig into it a bit. I know Mrs. Ryan often takes her horses out late in the evenings, so I thought she might have seen someone. Or you might."

They exchanged glances. "We haven't seen anyone at the beach," Emily began, she glanced at Sophie. "But..."

"Well," Sophie took over. "We did hear that Mr. Quinn that's staying at the cottage say something strange the other night. On the phone, we overheard him on our ride, he was talking about not having something yet, and he's a bit odd."

Oddsocks nodded.

"We know it's not much to go on," Jack put in. "But we thought we should say."

"Right, you are Jack," Inspector Oddsocks nodded. "Nothing too small to mention.

I'll keep an eye on the fellow, and you all keep an eye out for lights on the beach. If you see any lights call me right away, I want to get a look at whoever's going down there."

"We will," Emily promised. "Inspector? When was the last time someone saw the lights?"

"Oh, oh, well, there was a spate of reports before you found the brooch, and then nothing for a while, but they started up again last night. Strange though."

"What's strange?" Emily asked.

"Well, first reports were by the coast. This new lot are around the far end of the beach, more towards the village," he shook his head. "I'm still inclined to say it's a hiker enjoying the moonlit bay, but, I have to check these things, it is my duty after all."

"Big barn you said," Sophie nodded and the policeman headed away towards the larger of Mrs. Ryan's barns.

"Something weird is definitely going on," Jack whispered as Inspector Oddsocks disappeared. "I'm betting whoever stole the brooch is looking for the treasure."

"And maybe that tunnel we read about," Sophie added. "That's why they were at both ends of the beach."

"How would they know?" Emily asked. Sophie shrugged.

"I tell you one thing," Jack mused. "If someone was snooping around looking for a treasure, the best time to do anything about stealing it would be during the parade. That's what I'd do, use it as a distraction."

Emily and Sophie exchanged glances. "I think we better call for Conor on the way home. If you're right Jack we need to be ready for the weekend."

Chapter 12

Sophie handed Jack the little radio. "It's tuned into the same frequency as the stables one," she said.

"Your Mum didn't mind you taking it?" Conor asked glancing at the tavern radio.

Sophie shook her head. "I told her it was for safety reasons. You know what she's like with health and safety."

Conor smiled as he smoothed out a sheet of A3 paper on his bedroom floor. He'd drawn the village on it and marked the parade out in red marker.

"Alright, here's the plan," he glanced up at the others. "Most of the village will be busy from 8.30 a.m. when they start setting up the party here," he pointed to the green.

"That leaves the village pretty wide open."

"I'll be here," Jack pointed to the end of the village by the library. "Near the beach with Benji. We found a perfect hide spot in the dunes, lots of tall grass."

"Perfect," Conor nodded. "You'll have a good view of things up the street and the beach."

"I'll be at the pub," Sophie nodded pointing to her house. "I told Mum I have to sort out the costumes to take up to the stables, but I did it last night really. I put everything we need for the horses in my tack box. That way I can watch the centre of the village first thing."

"And Conor and I will get the ponies ready for the parade and then bring all three down to our house. There's that old tether post in the back we can tie up too. We can take it in turns to watch the ponies and this end of the village." Emily nodded.

"We know they can't be planning to drive away from the village itself during the parade," Conor put in.

"The road will be closed, but I heard that Quinn moved his car up to a spot by the church. He said it was to get it out of the way of the party, but..."

"But it would mean he could leave too," Emily nodded. "The church road is outside of the parade route, so Oddsock's won't close it."

"Exactly. He'll close the rest of the village off at 10.30 about half an hour before the parade. That's when most people will go home and change into their parade things."

"But we're in ours already," Emily pointed out. "So, we can stay watching."

Conor nodded. "We'll say we're riding the route one last time in costume to make sure the horses are comfortable. That way we can be out and about."

"What about the actual parade?" Jack asked. "I mean, we need to be in it."

"I thought about that," Conor nodded. "If it comes to it, we'll split up. Jack, you, and Emily will go towards the front of the parade, Sophie and I will hang back and go at the rear. Keep our eyes open and if we spot anyone, radio Mrs. Ryan. She always has her radio on her, and she can fetch Katie or Inspector Oddsocks."

"How do we explain splitting up?" Emily asked.

"We'll tell them Daisy is having an issue with Sophie's dress, she's always calmer with Rocky. They'll buy that," Conor nodded. "We can say she was a bit skittish on our trial ride and we want to keep her at the back where it's quieter."

"Ok, let's do it," Jack smiled.

They scrabbled up off the floor and looked at each other for a moment. Jack put his hand into the center of their little circle and they all followed suit.

"For St. Patrick's Day!" he said.

They all broke away and headed towards their positions. A strange mixture of excitement and worry filled Emily as she jogged down the stairs following her cousin. She glanced at Jack already peddling away on his bicycle, Benji at his feet. This St. Patrick's Day was proving very exciting already!

Chapter 13

Jack sat huddled in the tall grass of the dunes watching the distant street. Beside him Benji sat, his tongue lolling out, his gaze flitting between Jack and the beach.

Jack smiled at him and pulled a biscuit from his pocket passing half to the dog and popping the rest in his mouth.

"I'm not sure anyone would get up the street from the beach," Jack muttered around his biscuit. It was true. Mr. Lyle's old truck sat stubbornly blocking the road at the end of the village while chairs from the school were being stacked on it, to take up to the green.

Jack looked over at Benji with a sigh.

"I guess we're stuck for a while," he sighed. "We'd never get past that, between the chairs and the truck."

"Woof," Benji let out a little low woof. Jack glanced at him.

The labrador was staring towards the street. Jack followed his gaze and spotted a shape not far away huddled in the shadows of one of the cottages just past the truck.

Whoever it was had pulled a baseball cap firmly down on their head and was dressed in a long, dark coat. He almost completely blended in with the shadows.

Jack inched closer to see what the man was doing.

In the dim light, he could just make out the shape of a paper in the man's hands. Quickly he opened his backpack and pulled out his binoculars.

He scanned the figure, but the man had his back to Jack, so even with the binoculars he couldn't tell who it was.

The paper though, he could make that out. Jack took a sharp breath and fumbled to get his radio. He clicked the button twice before it worked.

"Conor, Emily, Sophie!"

"We're here, what is it, Jack?" Conor asked.

"I see someone, lurking down my end of the village. He's got a map," Jack replied.

"Who is it?" Emily asked.

"Can't tell, but I can see the map pretty well. It's old and it has the village drawn on it," Jack replied.

"Can you get closer?" Sophie asked.

"No way. Mr. Lyle's truck is blocking the road along with what looks like every chair in school. Mr. Lyle was stacking them, but he's stopped and nipped into Mrs. Quigley's with Miss O'Keefe. I'm guessing it's tea break."

"We're on our way, keep an eye on him," Conor said.

"Bring Daisy, I'll meet you out front," Sophie added.

Jack sat for a moment his binoculars trained on the man, and then, to his horror, the man began to move, crossing the street quickly, while the truck was unattended.

"We'll lose him," Jack huffed. "Come on."

Benji and Jack skidded and slid down the dunes onto the street below and jogged up the road.

Jack caught glimpses of the man as he walked further up the pathway, but by the time he had reached the truck, the man had disappeared.

"Oh no," Jack glanced at Benji. The dog managed to scramble under a stack of chairs, while Jack moved a few and slipped through the gap he made.

They were just about through the tangle of legs when Sophie, Emily, Conor, and the ponies arrived.

"Where is he?" Emily asked.

"I lost track of him," Jack huffed. "He crossed the road and seemed to disappear."

"We didn't pass anyone in a coat and baseball cap," Sophie pointed out.

"He must still be close," Conor nodded.

"He must have gone up the old alleyway," Jack nodded towards the narrow, overgrown alley at the side of the library.

"Let's go."

"The ponies won't fit," Sophie pointed out. "I'll wait with them, tether them to the old hitching post." She pointed to the little ringed post beside the library.

"Ok, keep your radio on," Conor handed her Rocky's reins.

The three children and Benji made their way along the narrow alleyway. The trees that grew beside the library had long ago consumed much of the space and since the lane was disused, they hadn't been trimmed. A waste of money the parish said. It was dark, shaded by both the leafy trees and the stone building. Jack pulled a flashlight from his bag and clicked it on, while Benji darted ahead. A second later they heard an echoing bark. Emily glanced at Jack. Why was there an echo?

The children broke through the tree line to see Benji standing wagging his tail next to a hole in the ground. A wooden door lay open, steps leading downward between them.

"Could be the old tavern cellar," Conor said.

They headed down the old stairs into what seemed to be a tunnel lined with brick. "Odd-looking cellar," Jack muttered.

"We should get Oddsocks," Emily said. "I'll radio Sophie, get her to take Daisy and find him."

Chapter 14

Emily followed Conor along the red brick tunnel, ahead of them she could make out a flickering light. She nudged Jack who nodded and lowered his torch a little. "It's got to be Mr. Quinn," Jack whispered to her. "Shh," Conor glanced at him.

They crept forward until Emily realised; they had reached a small doorway. They stepped through it together into a small dusty room. Cobwebs hung from old wooden beams of the ceiling and a few stray casks lay scattered on the floor.

They were in the old tavern basement beneath the library.

A figure by the far wall was pulling a wooden lid off a large wooden chest.

"It's over Mr. Quinn," Conor said. At the same time, Benji let out a low growl.

The man spun around and Emily gasped. In front of them stood Michael O'Leary. In one hand he held the silver brooch, and the other was filled with golden coins. Several more coins spilled from the little strong box behind him, dropping to the floor with a tinkling metallic sound.

"Now, it's not what it looks like..." he said.

"It looks like you're a thief!" Jack replied.

Benji growled again and took a step forward. In a fluid movement, Michael stuffed the gold coins into his pockets and pulled a latch Emily hadn't even noticed by his shoulder. With a thump and a cloud of dust a trap door, with wooden steps attached to it dropped open. Michael leapt for the opening, disappearing through the hazy cloud of dirt.

"After him!" Conor coughed.

They surged forward rushing up the steps into the library. Emily looked around herself and realised they were in one of the storerooms at the back of the building.

"That way," she pointed to a door behind them and they rushed for it.

They darted through the rooms of the library, catching glimpses of Michael's long dark coat as they ran. Jack pulled the radio out of his pocket, fumbling with it as he tried to contact Sophie while still running.

Michael burst through the front door of the library onto the empty street, the children not long behind him. Emily quickly realised that people must have gone to change ready for the parade as the street was empty. She looked in both directions and spotted Michael making for the beach as fast as he could run.

"He's going to the beach!" she yelled and they set off running.

"Sophie! Sophie!!" Jack was saying. Emily only half made out Sophie's voice as she reached Basil and scooped up her reins. Conor paused to look at her.

"We're faster on the ponies," she said and he went to grab Rocky.

"We found him, it's Michael, get Oddsocks!" Jack yelled down the radio as he ran further down the street to retrieve his bicycle, Benji running after him.

Michael was already running along the sand halfway across the beach when Conor and Emily caught up with Jack on his bike.

"He has a boat!" Jack yelled as they trotted past. "I saw it through my binoculars."

Emily glanced at Conor. "We might not catch him, even on the ponies."

They set off as fast as they could the horses struggling to canter on the soft sand before the firmer ground by the shore. Emily could see the boat now, and Michael running close to it. They were going to lose him, even Basil wasn't that fast. She felt her heart sink for a moment.

Then, to her surprise, a red blur dashed in front of Michael.

The man stumbled, tripping over Benji and landing face-first in the sand.

"Go!" Conor called.

Michael O'Leary was staggering to his feet when Conor and Emily arrived. Basil snorted loudly at him, and Benji growled.

They stood between him and the boat, the red-haired man turned preparing to run the other way only to see Sophie galloping towards him on Daisy, Jack, Oddsocks, and Katie behind her on their bicycles.

"It's all over," Conor said to him. He glanced at Emily. "I think there really must be a curse. It certainly brought bad luck to him."

Emily smiled. "In the form of a red labrador dog. Well done Benji, you've saved the day!"

Chapter 15

"It's quite something you found here," Inspector Oddsocks said as he looked around the cellar.

"That it is, that it is," Bones nodded staring around himself as the children smiled at each other. "And this is the treasure, for sure."

He looked over the chest still perched on the counter where Michael had left it. "Incan gold," he shook his head.

"I wonder how Michael knew about it?" Conor asked.

"I think I can answer that," Bones looked over at him.

"You see, I found another telling of the tale of the night the Silver Serpent sank. It mentions the owner of the tavern as one Niall O'Leary."

"That's Michael's name," Emily said.

"And he did say he was looking for information about his ancestors," Sophie added.

"Yes, well, he can explain it all to me," Inspector Oddsocks huffed.

"What happens to the treasure now?" Conor asked glancing at the glittering chest of gold.

"I'll have to take it into Galway headquarters. I expect they'll send it to the national museum for examination," Oddsocks replied.

"That doesn't seem very fair," Jack put in. "Not when we found it in the village. It should go to the museum here, it would be a great tourist attraction."

"Oh, now hold on," Bones smiled.

"While I appreciate your bold suggestion young Jack, I don't think I have the security for such a fine treasure or the longing for a curse. I would be obliged if perhaps I could keep the map you found on that fella though and maybe the brooch. A bit of the legend to hold on to."

"I should think that would be fair," Inspector Oddsocks nodded.

"I will suggest it when I hand it over. Perhaps a letter from yourself, and the children might carry some favour in that direction too?" he added. The children smiled at each other and nodded.

"Oh no!" Sophie put in suddenly. "We forgot about the parade, we'll miss it!"

Emily felt her heart sink a little. It had been so exciting finding the treasure and catching Michael she'd forgotten all about the parade.

"Don't worry," Bones said.

"I was with Mrs. Ryan when young Sophie came rushing to find the inspector here. I have a feeling she may well have delayed the proceedings a little on your behalf, but you had better get moving." The children smiled at each other and at Bones.

Inspector Oddsocks cleared his throat. "Go along now then," he said.

"Mr. O'Brien and I will take this all down to the police station for safekeeping until I can transport it. And I think a little chat with that Michael fellow is in order."

"If it isn't too much trouble," Bones said closing the lid on the chest. "I should like to hear that story myself."

The children darted up the stairs through the trapdoor to the library leaving the treasure behind. Outside they could hear the band starting to warm up at the top of the street.

"We better hurry," Conor said untying Rocky from the tether post. "We still need to put on our outfits."

They hurried up the village to find Mrs. Ryan standing at the head of the parade holding their things. She smiled at them.

"I don't know what adventures you've been on, but if you want to be in the parade, you have five minutes," she said handing Sophie her large green skirt.

"And I want all the details afterward," she added as she took hold of Basil so that Emily could pull on her green dress.

"There's a change of route too. Something about Inspector Oddsocks needing to open the road to move something. The party will be on the beach, so the route will now go straight there."

She looked flustered.

"Lord knows how we moved all those chairs to the shore, or how we'll move them back," she shook her head.

Emily jumped up on Basil beside her cousin while Sophie mounted Daisy and turned her around so she was following them alongside Jack on his bicycle.

Even Benji had been given a green ribbon around his neck. He looked very proud of himself.

The band struck up a tune and the parade, full of happy adults and children, and complete with banners and bunting began to wind its way slowly through the streets towards the beach.

"What a day," Conor smiled.

Emily nodded. "Treasure, parades, hidden tunnels, I bet this is the most exciting St. Patrick's Day the village ever saw!"

She paused for a second as she caught sight of Quinn in the crowd, he looked nervous and she frowned.

"You do think Michael was working alone, don't you?" she asked her cousin.

Chapter 16

Emily slid down off Basil and wrapped her arms around his neck patting him. Beside her Conor jumped down from Rocky. Mrs. Ryan came across the sand towards them smiling.

"I know you planned to take the ponies back right after the parade and come back to the party, but I'd wait a little," she smiled and glanced over at Bones who was talking animatedly to the parish chairman.

"I wonder what that's about," Jack mused as he propped his bicycle against the dunes and slipped a leash onto Benji. The lab was almost never on a lead, but with this much food and people about they'd thought it a good plan.

"Ladies and gentlemen," Mr. Doyle, the parish chairman clapped his hands together and everyone slowly stopped chatting and turned towards him.

"Thank you. Well, what a wonderful parade!" The crowd clapped.

"And thank you to the ladies of the parish committee for so hurriedly organising the party to be moved."

There was another round of clapping. "I suppose you are wondering why we needed to move the party.

Well, I can tell you our own Inspector Oddsocks and Officer Catchem have not only apprehended the brooch thief, but also recovered a great treasure hidden in our own village." There were gasps, but the chairmen held up his hand.

"None of which they could have done without the help of four special members of our community." Bones lent in and whispered something to the chairman, Mr. Doyle sighed.

"Make that eight members of our community. He waved the children towards him. "Children, em, ponies and dog."

They glanced at each other and then walked over the sand towards him. He smiled at them as they approached and the crowd cheered and clapped.

"Well done," Mr. Doyle said shaking each of their hands.

Afterward, several people crowded around to ask them what had happened, but Emily only half heard their questions, she had noticed Mr. Quinn wandering along the beach looking more and more nervous.

She nudged Jack and he nodded. "I know," he said.

"Did Michael tell you how he knew about the treasure?" Conor was asking Bones.

"And where he got the map?" Sophie put in.

"Yes he did. He spilled the beans as soon as he was at the station. Seems he was going through his late grandfather's belongings and he stumbled over an old journal kept by an ancestor of his that ran the tavern. It detailed the night that the Silver Serpent was wrecked and the tale of the treasure.

It went on though. It seems the priest at the time was so concerned about the curse, that he retrieved the treasure with the help of O'Leary.

The priest hid it in the tavern cellar, intent on no one knowing where it was, but O'Leary it seems wasn't so sure it should never be found.

So when the priest asked him to hide and burry the silver serpent key that unlocked the strongbox, he also hid a map to the treasure's location close by in a silver tin. That was what O'Leary was searching for with the metal detector. Only you found the brooch first."

"But he found the tin," Conor nodded.

"Aye," Bones nodded.

Emily frowned. "Did he say if he worked alone?"

"Didn't mention anyone else, why?"

"Nothing," Emily glanced at Quinn.

"Would you look at that," Bones glanced out over the steadily rolling sea.

"The sun is going down. I think we should see about lighting a few fires, keep folks warm and maybe make this parade and party a bit of a beach do. What do you think?"

"Sounds good to me," Mr. Doyle replied from beside him.

They drifted away together towards the food tables and Mr. Doyle called several people over to help collect wood.

Emily was distracted though by the sight of Mr. Quinn headed towards the dunes, his phone in his hands. The children glanced at each other and followed him. Even from a few feet away, they could hear him talking in a hushed voice.

"No, no, it's not here, it was supposed to be here. Where is it? No, it's not on the beach!"

"What are you looking for?" Jack asked.

Quinn froze. He looked over at them and then sighed, hanging up the phone. "A boat if you must know," he huffed.

"The one that was at the end of the beach?" Jack asked.

Quinn's eyes lit up. "It's here? Where?"

"I think Katie moved it," Conor replied. "After she caught that fellow Michael O'Leary you're working with trying to escape in it."

"Working with?" Quinn looked confused.

Miss. Flaherty walked up to them, her smile turning into a frown. "What's going on?"

Quinn sighed and then smiled a little sadly. "I seem to have given these children the impression I'm treasure hunting."

"You're not?" Conor asked, confused.

"What about the boat?" Emily asked.

"What boat?" asked Miss. Flaherty. The sun was really setting now, casting pink hues across the beach.

Quinn sighed again. "I charted a boat, it's out by the old harbour and there should be a small row boat here to take us to it." He shook his head.

"I was going to take us out to the Aran Islands, where your family are from. It seemed like the right place to do this."

He bent down on one knee and pulled a box with a ring in it, out of his pocket.

Miss. Flaherty's hands flew to her face and she gasped. "Fiona Flaherty, will you marry me?"

"Yes," she replied with a little gasp.

A cheer went up from the crowd behind them and Mr. Quinn stood up smiled and twirling her around in the sand.

"That explains it," Conor looked at Emily. She smiled back at him and nodded.

"I guess," she said as Mr. Quinn lowered Fiona to the sand again. "You weren't talking about the brooch that night we heard you on the phone outside the pub."

He frowned and then laughed.

"No," he chuckled. "I was on the phone with my friend. He sent my grandmother's heirloom ring to me. I forgot to pack it and we were worried it had been lost by the courier."

They all laughed a little before the village flooded in to congratulate the couple and see the sparkling diamond ring.

Emily stood back with her friends watching as the sun sank further over the Atlantic, its long rays of golden light playing on the sands.

It really had been an exciting adventure. And as she stared out over the ocean with her friends by her side, she wondered what other adventures they would have.

She had a feeling that their next adventure wasn't too far away...

Enjoy the next books in the series

www.elaineheneybooks.com

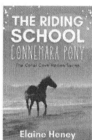
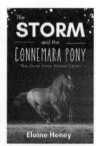

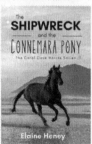

Made in the USA
Monee, IL
16 February 2025

12367271R00067